Jan Kjær & Merlin P. Mann

TAYNIKMA

Book 2: The Rats

Young World Digital

MMVIII

TAYNIKMA
Book 2: The Rats
(Original title: Rotterne)

Translated by Merlin P. Mann

© Jan Kjær & Merlin P. Mann
© This edition Young World Digital Ltd, London, U.K.

ISBN 978-0-9558337-1-7
First edition

Published by:
Young World Digital Ltd • PO Box 6268 • London W1A 2HE
www.youngworlddigital.com

Printed and bound in Great Britain in 2008
by Stanley L. Hunt (Printers) Ltd, Rushden, Northants

British Library Cataloguing in Publication Data available.

TAYNIKMA
Book 1: Master Thief
Book 2: The Rats
Book 3: Tower of the Sun
Book 4: The Lost Catacombs
Book 5: The Secret Arena
Book 6: Duel of the Clans
Book 7: Henzel's Ambush
Book 8: The Forest of Shadows
Book 9: The Fortress of Light
Book 10: The Final Battle

www.taynikma.co.uk

Sarratum Mountains

Fortress of Light

The Tamharo Woods

The Forest of Shadows

Korsay Village

Zirania

Forest of the Knomes

City of Klanaka

Abnepolis

Mkaza

TAYCLANIA

The Land of Tayclania

South of the mountains, north of the sea lies Tayclania.

For hundreds of years it was a haven for merchants, craftsmen and scholars. A land ruled by four clans: The Sun, The Moon, The Mountain and The River Clans.

Each clan had its own deities and powers. The Sun Clan had the healing powers of light, the Moon Clan had the protection of shadow, the Mountain Clan had raw strength, and the River Clan had wisdom.

Even though it was a land of plenty, quarrels began to break out between the clans. The quarrels lead to fights. The fights lead to war.

A treaty was signed, but few believed the four clans could rule together again.

Peace was short-lived. A sorceress murdered three champions from each clan and from their souls she created 12 invincible knights: the Sentinels. Soon all of Tayclania had to bow to her rule and she became The Empress.

The clans were outlawed, the borders were closed and The Empress imposed the Law of the Sun. She declared that only by having just one deity could the land live in peace and harmony. A brief uprising was attempted by the clans but was easily crushed by the Sentinels.

Soon the rule of the immortal Empress of Light will have lasted for 100 years.

KOTO

He is 14 and training with Master Gekko to become a thief. He has a special ability with shadows. Thinks the best of people, but is slowly learning his lessons in the big city of Klanaka.

MASTER GEKKO

Has lived longer than most, but is still strong and agile. He is a master thief and has been looking for the right apprentice for ages. Now he has found Koto.

SNEAK

A tall kid with yellow eyes and a long tail. He leads a gang of thieves called The Rats and is always looking for a big score. Often caught, but always manages to buy his way out of jail.

BULLY

Sneak's trusty companion. Bully's family were travelling folk, but he ended up in the streets of Klanaka. Sneak gave him shelter and ever since he feels he owes his life to The Rats – even though he actually doesn't like stealing.

The story so far ...

What's happening, Master Kayton?

Koto and his parents will be home-
less unless they get 300 coins
before the first snow falls. Koto
travels the dangerous route to the
city of Klanaka to sell an old heirloom.
He only completes his journey due to
his special shadow powers.

In Klanaka he is cheated out of his treasure by the thieves
Sneak and Bully – and he ends up being arrested by the
nefarious Captain Henzel, leader of
the city guards.

I really saved your neck, boy!

SPEAK UP!

The master thief Gekko notices Koto's
special powers and buys his way out of jail. He sends
Koto on a dangerous mission to steal two scrolls from
Captain Henzel.

Koto barely gets away, but
Master Gekko is convinced of his abilities. Koto becomes
his apprentice.

... your dad will never have to worry about Lord Tuskan again!

Book 2: The Rats

The Eeks

Koto couldn't read, but the many signs with skulls on them were not hard to understand. This was forbidden territory. Forbidden and dangerous.

As always Master Gekko had told him very little about the mission. "Find the black ship. Locate a small chest with the drawing of a lotus flower. And remember: use the shadows! Danger lurks everywhere!"

Koto jumped aboard an old ship wreck with torn, black sails. The slight wobble was a bit unnerving.

The Hull gave a scary creak for every step he took. »I wonder how much longer this ship will hold?« thought Koto. That question was answered quickly ...

Koto spotted the mast's shadow on the deck. »TENE-GARA!" he yelled and the shadow became a sticky rope in his hands.

»I hope I can hold on to this,« he gasped as he fell through the deck.

The air of the cargo hold was dense and the smell was unbearable. Koto looked down. By swinging the shadow rope he could swing into a heap of sacks.

Eeww! Landing in the stinking, rotting corn sacks was no fun, but at least he was unhurt. He got to his feet and brushed off the dirt and slime. The smell would be harder to lose.

»I can't breathe down here,« thought Koto. »I'd better find that stupid chest fast.« He looked around. Large boxes were hanging on old ropes from the ceiling. They wouldn't hold much longer. He had to hurry.

Koto looked around confused by the weird sounds. Eek! Eek! It came from all over – and it was closing in! Koto took a frightened step back, as a horde of small, ugly heads appeared from the sacks. »Holy rock slide!« gasped Koto.

»I need a weapon,« thought Koto and looked desperately for something to fight off the critters with. He pulled a door from the rotting closet.

The little creeps didn't expect any resistance and pulled back quickly. Koto let go of the closet door and turned his attention to the shelves. Pots, pans, tins and – yes! A small chest with a lotus flower. »That's it!« cheered Koto forgetting everything about the vile rodents. »Easy job, this!«

But the critters had not given up. In fact even more of them had joined the pack. They were too many to be brushed off now. What was it Gekko always said? "Use the shadow!" A shadow rope wouldn't help, but what about a shadow shield?

»Tene-fa- ... TENE-FALANX!« cried Koto just as the giant pack of eeks jumped towards him.

Koto was safe – for now! The eeks had not given up yet. They all closed in on Koto's shield and began to shriek louder and louder. Koto knew the voice of one eek could stun a small animal. He wondered what the cries of a pack this large could do to him ...

EEK! EEEK! EEEEEK!

Koto was getting dizzy from the sounds and his arms began to hurt. He could hardly feel his fingers anymore and his shadow powers were getting weaker.

I can't hold up the shield ...

Koto's heart beat quickly as the shield began to crack. He had to do something now. What about that shadow whip Gekko had told him about? Maybe it could hold the eeks at a distance? Koto mumbled the words ... but nothing happened! »I'm ... too weak ...« thought Koto. Then he noticed a crate hanging right above the eeks. If only he could make it fall, it would crush the creeps. He dropped the shield and grabbed a large kitchen knife from the closet behind him.

I only get one shot at this!

It worked! The knife barely grazed the rope, but luckily that was enough. The crate thundered down on the pack of eeks – and broke right through the bottom of the hull!

The eeks jumped away in panic as the water rushed into the ship with great force. Koto ran to the hole in the deck.

»How am I going to get up there?« he gasped. The hull was shaking violently. »Te-ne ... Ga-ra ...« Koto tried to make a shadow rope, but he was totally exhausted.

»TENE-GARA!« Koto heard a voice from above and a shadow rope appeared through the hole. Koto got hold of it in the nick of time. He was close to fainting but held on the best he could.

»Master Gekko!« Koto said under his breath. »You saved my life ...«

Where's the chest?

Err – I found it ... but ...

Koto pointed into the water.

»For crying out …!« barked Gekko. »That was lotus tea from Annat! No one has been able to get it since the Empress closed the borders – and I just ran out!«

»Tea?!« said Koto. »Did I risk my life for a chest of tea?«

»Risk your life?!« snapped Gekko. »If only you had used your powers, you would have risked nothing!«

»But I'm not that strong!« protested Koto.

»Nonsense! You weren't that focused!« said Gekko.

Koto got back up on his feet with a snarl.

»What do you know about that?« he yelled. »I'm doing my best, but there's just no pleasing you whatever I do!«

Gekko watched Koto silently for a moment.

»You don't lack strength,« he said quietly. »You lack faith. Faith in yourself and your skills. You just need more training.«

A lot more training …

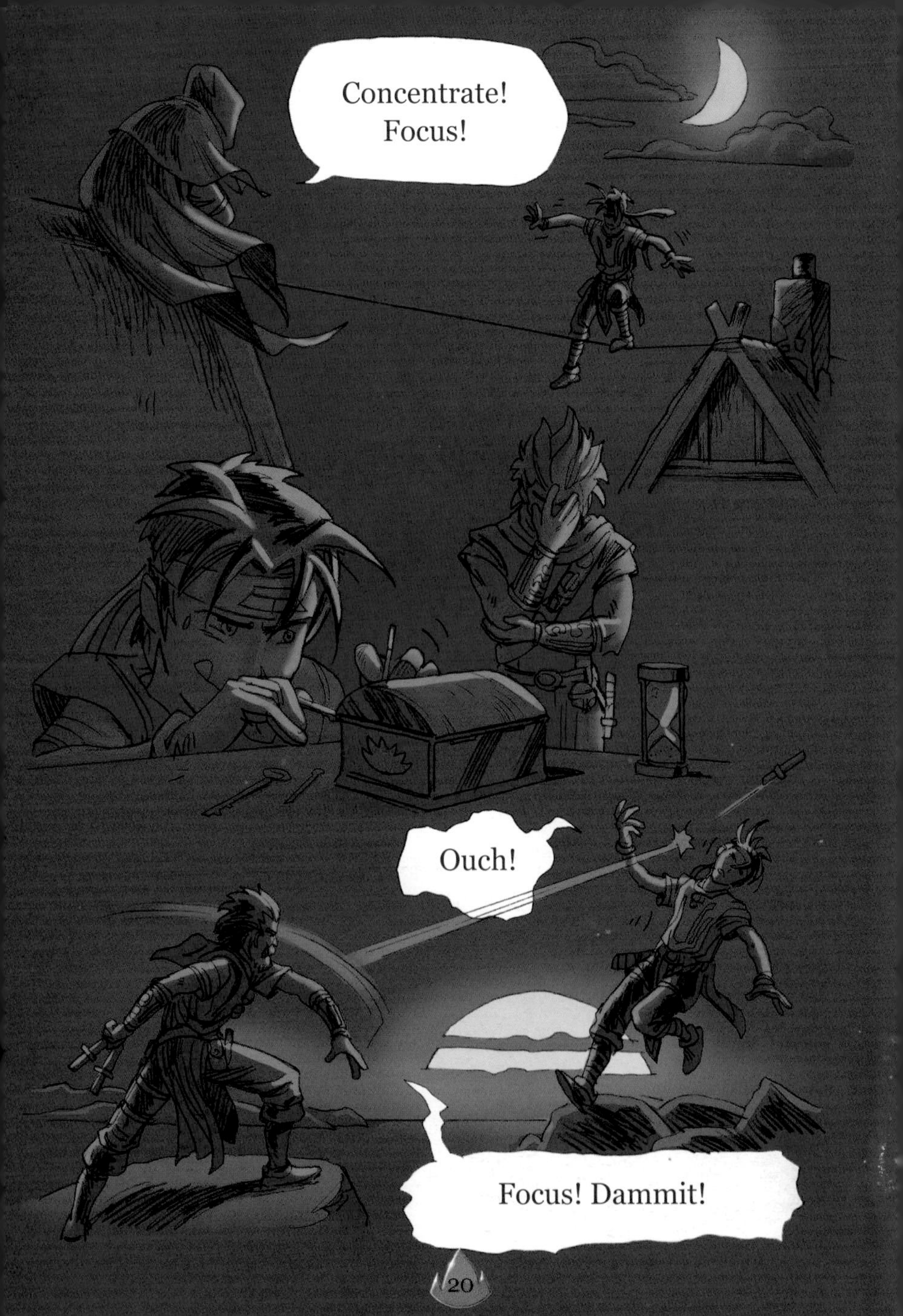
Concentrate!
Focus!
Ouch!
Focus! Dammit!

Koto was totally exhausted when he came back to Gekko's attic that night. The training had been tough, and he never knew if Gekko was happy with him.

»You're getting better, Koto,« said Gekko and handed him the water skin. »It's time ...«

Is my training complete?

Am I a thief now?

Are you mad?

Training a thief takes years!

»But we don't have that time. Your abilities are needed now.« Koto had no idea what Gekko was talking about, but that was no surprise. Gekko never told him anything. It was just training all day and then back to the attic for a few hours of sleep.

»What do we have to do?« asked Koto as he washed his face.

»We? 'We' don't have to do anything. YOU have to!« said Gekko. »YOU have to get your nikma back!«

Koto had thought about the valuable heirloom many times, but it was in the hands of The Rats, a gang of thieves. The toughest gang in Klanaka.

»The Rats are only dangerous in numbers. On their own they are nothing but simple pick-pockets!« said Gekko. »You just need to sneak into their cave and snatch the nikma. A great beginner's mission!«

But that's madness!

»If I break into their territory they will have all the advantages,« said Koto.

»Not if you're well prepared,« said Gekko. »I've got a small surprise for you.«

»A surprise? What is it?« asked Koto as Gekko pulled something from an old chest.

»Your thief's gear Koto!« smiled Gekko. »It has everything a thief needs for breaking into a place of brutal, blood-thirsty bullies! Put it on now, so we can get going right away!«

The Rats' Nest

The stench of the sewers had numbed Koto's sense of smell, and now he could actually breathe without getting nauseous. The sewers consisted of an endless maze of canals and tunnels, many of them hidden by heaps of junk or collapsed ceilings. Without the map that Gekko had given him, Koto would never have found the way to the Rat's hideout.

That's the door!

Koto folded the map. »All I have to do now is pick the lock ...«

He tip-toed up to the heavy old door and took out his lock-picking tools. He crouched in front of the lock and was just about to go to work ...

CLANK! Koto's heart almost stopped as someone unlocked the door from the inside!

»Holy goat! Now I'm in trouble!«

The door was opening, and Koto had no time to escape. Just then the light from within the door caused a shadow to appear above the opening. Koto grabbed it instantly and pulled himself up on the crossbeam. The door was open and someone came out right underneath him. He had to be quiet as a mouse.

Hear somethin'?

Nah! Nuthin' but us Rats down 'ere!

»Rats? They sure look like it,« thought Koto. »If only they would also run off like rats. I don't know how much longer I can keep from falling ...«

Then the "rat" accidentally kicked Koto's lock-picking tools that he had left on the floor!

Who has lost his tools?!

»That has to be Bully, « laughed the other thief. »He's not the quickest rat in the sewer ...«

Koto's legs were starting to ache. The crossbeam was very narrow and there was nothing for him to hold on to. He'd slip any instance now!

The first "rat" picked up the tools and looked at them closely. »That's strange! « he said suspiciously. »I've never seen this kind of lock-pick before! «

Something's not right ...

Now's the time to test my equipment!

With one hand Koto carefully pulled out two capsules from a pocket inside his outfit.

The gas instantly knocked both "rats" unconscious. »I ought to push you into the canal,« thought Koto. »But there's enough rubbish down there already!«

»They are not going to get up for a while,« thought Koto as he picked up the rat's key. He turned to the door again and this time he had no trouble getting inside the Rat's nest.

Behind the door was a small room with a small chair and a couple of old chairs. A fire was burning in the middle of the room and the light revealed a lot of dug-out corridors leading deeper into the nest.

»I have no clue which way to go,« Koto sighed. »They all look dirty and uninviting!« Was he supposed to simply stroll down a random corridor without knowing what was at the other end? What advice would Gekko give at a time like this?

»Focus! Have faith in yourself!« said Koto in Gekko's voice. »Like that's going to help!«

Koto had already wasted too much time. A voice he knew all too well cried out behind him:

Look Bully!
We've got guests!

Huh-whoops!
That's the
farm boy!

»Yup,« said Sneak and aimed his crossbow right at Koto. »We should give him a warm welcome ...«

»I want my nikma back ...« said Koto, but Sneak didn't even bother to answer him.

»Welcome to the Rat's Nest ...« laughed Sneak viciously, as Koto fell to the floor clutching his injured shoulder. »Pick him up, Bully. We don't want that goat's dropping lying around!«

Koto could hardly breathe, as Bully pulled him up and swung him over one shoulder. The pain was unbearable and Koto was too exhausted to fight Bully. »I better pretend to be unconscious,« thought Koto.

»Huh-why did you shoot him?« mumbled Bully. »He wasn't about to attack ...«

»Shoot first, questions later,« laughed Sneak as he headed down one of the corridors. »Come on, Bully! We might as well use the kid for something!«

Bully had a hard time keeping up with quick Sneak, but soon they reached a cave with a huge ancient well.

»We have to feed Mamma,« giggled Sneak and pointed into the well. »She wants her meat absolutely fresh. Nothing better than a live steak!«

Bully hesitated. Koto was finally catching his breath and he focused on drawing enough shadow power from the darkness. This was his final chance.

Huh-whoa!

I don't want to get too close. I could fall into The Deep!

Shut up, fatso!

Throw in farm boy. NOW!

Bully was mumbling something, but he clearly didn't have the guts to stand up to Sneak. He slowly walked over to the edge of the well.

»Focus!« thought Koto. He could feel the shadow power stirring within him, and now he just needed to control it – not with his fear, but with his will. Just like Gekko had taught him. Or else he would probably be falling to a fate worse than death!

»Do it, Bully!« hissed Sneak. »Think about poor Mamma! How hungry she must be …«

Bully was just about to let Koto fall from his shoulder when …

TENE-GARA!

SNEEEAK!

If I go down, so does Bully!

For several very long seconds all he could hear was Bully sobbing. The big kid was obviously very scared of what was at the bottom of the well. Sneak didn't say anything. He just smiled and walked closer.

»I'm warning you, Sneak!« said Koto. »I'll take him down with me!«

»Huh-he's serious!« whined Bully shaking like a little puppy.

»Well,« shrugged Sneak …

I guess that's fair.

Nothing's free …

Then he pulled the shadow rope from the wall and Koto and Bully tumbled down into the darkness!

The Deep

They fell through the darkness straight into a deep underground lake. Koto quickly got his head above water, but Bully was in a panic.

HUH-HEEELP!

Koto swam to the shore of the lake and with the shadow rope still hanging on to Bully he could pull the panicky boy with him.

»Huh-huh ...« sobbed Bully all curled up on the ground. »You saved my life! Th-thank you!«

»You were about to throw me in!« said Koto.

»And I'm really sorry about that!« said Bully and looked up with sad eyes. »Boy, it's way too dark down here!«

Just stick with me!

Bully walked all the way over to Koto and carefully put his hand on his shoulder. »You're hurt,« he mumbled. »Let me get that thing out of there ...«

It was painful, but Bully managed to pull the crossbow bolt from Koto's shoulder. Then he tore patches from his clothes and made a bandage.

»Thank you, Bully!« said Koto. »Now we just have to find our way out of here.« He spotted an opening at the far end of the cave and pointed.

»Huh-must be one of the old tunnels!« gasped Bully.

We dug into them a year ago.

That's when we ran into ... Mamma!

»Who's mum lives down here?« asked Koto.

»It was just a name Sneak came up with,« whispered Bully. »She's actually a fierce monster. If you fall into The Deep, she'll eat you up!«

No need to stick around then!

Huh-wait! Don't go!

»The tunnel is even darker than the cave!« said Bully. »I can't see a thing in there!«

Koto looked back at Bully. It was strange to see such a strong, burly boy so helpless. »I'll tie your tail around my waist,« said Koto. »That way you can feel where I am at all times!«

Bully looked down. »It's actually not a real tail,« he said. »It's just something I sew onto my trousers to look like the other Rats ...«

»I'll still be able to lead you through the dark, if we're tied together,« smiled Koto and grabbed Bully's "tail". Then he walked inside the dark tunnel.

»Huh-did you hear something?« asked Bully. Koto stopped. He didn't hear anything at first, but then he noticed a high-pitched shriek. A sound he had heard just recently: Eek! Eek! EEEEK!

»They're coming straight at us,« said Koto and got ready for the attack – but Bully tore off his "tail", turned around and ran back out into the cave.

But Bully was gone and Koto had to follow him. He just barely made it out of the tunnel before a horde of eeks came bursting out like a flood. Koto expected them to attack – but instead they kept running through the cave. They were obviously in a panicked flight.

ZEEEK

HUH-OOH!

The giant eek came out into the cave while tasting the air with its tongue. It noticed Bully and walked with heavy steps towards the crack in the wall. It was as if it could smell his fear!

»Hello! Over here, you pile of muck!« yelled Koto and threw a couple of rocks at the enormous body. It was like throwing peas at a stone wall, but at least Koto got the attention of the giant eek. It turned towards him instead of Bully – and Koto could almost see a smile on the monster's terrible face.

»Whoops!« said Koto. »Now what?«

»ZEEEK!« it hissed and opened its jaw. The razor-sharp teeth were glistening with yellow saliva. Then it jumped towards Koto!

WATCH OUT!

It spits acid!

The giant eek spewed out thick, yellow goo from the tip of its ugly tongue. If Bully was right about it being acid, Koto had better get out of the way. One drop and he would be done for!

»TENE-FALANX!« Just as the acid was about to hit him, Koto put up a shadow shield – and that saved him! The acid bounced off the shield, and that gave Koto an idea!

»Try that again, you beast!« yelled Koto. »Let's see one more of your acid attacks!«

ZEEEK!

The giant eek shot off another load of goo, and this time Koto managed to make the acid bounce right back at the eyes of the beast!

Let's go, Bully!

ZEEK! ZEEK! The giant eek was blinded but not about to give up its prey! It gave a series of high-pitched shrieks – and suddenly it seemed to know exactly where Koto was!

It uses the screens to find its way!

»Just like the bats back home in Korsay!« thought Koto. The giant eek was headed straight for him with its constant shrieking. It swung its huge claws, and Koto realized there was no way his shadow shield would be able to withstand them.

»I have to get away!« thought Koto. But how? He looked around in panic, but then he noticed the many stalactites hanging from the ceiling high above. Maybe he could get hold of one and get out of the creature's reach? He would have to use the shadow whip that Gekko had taught him about.

But what were the words ...?

»TENE- ... TENE-SORA!« yelled Koto and a long whip appeared from the shade into his hand. He threw it up towards the stalactites – and it actually stuck!

»Holy cave troll!« gasped Koto. »Why is it always such a close call?!« He wiped the sweat from his forehead, as the giant eek tried to locate Koto with its terrible shrieks.

»Tene-gara!« said Koto and turned some shadow into a rope that he could tie himself to the rock with. He was at safe distance from the beast – at least for now. But his shadow power wouldn't hold up forever.

Bully!

You have to distract it, so I can get back down!

But Bully didn't move from the crack in the wall. He was shaking with fear. »Huh-I wanna go home!« he hollered. Koto was on his own.

ZEEK! Suddenly the shrieks of the giant eek became more and more fierce. Koto looked down. It couldn't reach him, so what was it up to? Then Koto heard a creaking sound from the stalactites. Little cracks appeared one by one.

If this one breaks …

… I'll be headed right down its belly!

CRRACKK! Small stalactites began dropping to the floor. »I just have to hold on,« thought Koto. »And hope for the best …«

Koto closed his eyes and sent out a prayer to every helping spirit he knew. Then everything came down in a huge crash!

»I'm done for!« he gasped, and then the fall knocked the air from his lungs. For a long time he couldn't even open his eyes. »What happened?« whispered Koto. He was lying in a big pile of broken stalactites on top of the unconscious beast!

Ha!

She wasn't expecting that much to fall!

Koto had bruises all over, but at least it was better than ending up in an acid-filled belly.

»Come on, Bully!« said Koto to the surprised boy. »We had better find a tunnel that leads out of here – before the beast wakes up!«

Bully looked with disbelief at the monster beneath the rocks. »Huh-whoa!« he said. »You're the toughest farm boy I have ever seen!«

Koto and Bully moved quickly through the tunnels and soon they found a narrow corridor leading back up to the Rat's nest. It was blocked, but Bully got out his axe and started hacking at the barricade. He was strong and eager, and soon they could both squeeze their way through.

That's twice you've saved my life!

We did it together, Bully!

It's okay!

Ouch! My shoulder! You can let go now ...

»Now, let's go find that thing that was stolen from you!« said Bully. »Follow me!«

Taynikma

»What if anyone sees us?« asked Koto as Bully led the way through the small corridors of the Rat's secret hide-out.

»I don't belong here with the Rats anymore!« said Bully. »Stupid Sneak! He always made me do wrong things – but now that's all over!«

Koto couldn't help smiling. Even though Bully had helped Sneak steal his nikma, it wasn't hard for him to forgive the big bear cub!

In there!

That's Sneak's quarters. The padlock is on, so he must be out ...

Luckily Koto still had his lock-picking tools.

Huh-you are much better than Sneak at that!

Koto pushed open the heavy door. The room inside wasn't that big, but with the mess in there it would take ages to find anything. But Koto didn't hesitate. He began looking feverishly through the piles of junk. No nikma ...

Maybe you should check his secret locker?

»He has a secret locker?« asked Koto and gave Bully an annoyed look. »Where?«

Bully climbed a junk-pile and below the ceiling pushed a fake piece of wall aside. A small locker door appeared. »That's it!« cheered Koto. Bully pulled it open and ...

CRASHHH! CLANGGG! BOINGGG! Heaps of stolen goods fell out over Bully and onto the floor. Koto quickly looked through the goods and yes! There it was. Koto's nikma.

But they had made too much noise ...

What the ...?

Has Mamma
lost her appetite?

Sneak put down the cage he was carrying and made sure the door was blocked. »You tried to kill us!« sneered Koto holding the nikma. »Bully, let's take him! We're two against one!«

Bully jumped at Sneak, but the skinny boy was a lot faster. He stepped aside and caught Bully in his net. Bully was all tangled up and fell to the floor. »Huh-I'm stuck!« he cried.

»Now it's your turn, farm boy,« said Sneak as he picked a broken table leg from the floor. Koto tried to get past Sneak – but the Rat was quick. Very quick!

»Too slow, you loser!« laughed Sneak and struck Koto right inside the knees. The pain made Koto collapse.

»The s-shadow power ...« thought Koto, as he crimped on the floor. »Focus your shadow power ...«

But everything was spinning inside his head. What could he make? A shadow rope? A whip? A shield? He just couldn't focus.

UMPF! Sneak kicked Koto hard, and he lost his breath for a moment.

»I'm actually pleased that you survived the fall into The Deep,« snapped Sneak.

Sneak stepped arrogantly closer with his knife ready. Suddenly Koto felt a small jolt coming from the nikma on the floor. He looked at it and – CLAKK! It was open. »Shadow power,« he thought and reached out.

CLINK! The nikma placed itself right on his wrist.
»What's going on?« said a confused Sneak. Koto didn't even know himself, but as soon as the nikma was on his arm he felt a force like never before!

You don't have to get up!

The power of the mysterious shadow blade hit Sneak so hard that he was flung through the air. He landed heavily on the floor right beside Bully, who was still caught in the net.

»So farm boy is your new pal, huh?« sneered Sneak and grabbed Bully's neck. »Lose the sword, Koto!«

It was no empty threat, and Koto had to let go of the shadow blade – but instead of falling to the ground it just disappeared into thin air.

»Leave Bully alone!« yelled Koto.

Drop the knife and let him go!

»You're unarmed now, you fool! And Blubber Boy needs to be taught a lesson for his treason!« said Sneak with a vicious smile. He held up his knife ...

»TENE-SORA!« cried Koto and a whip shot from the nikma – stronger and faster than any Gekko had ever created. SWISHHH! It hit Sneak's wrist with such force and precision that he had to let go of the knife screaming with pain. Bully quickly got hold of it and cut his way out of the net, while Sneak was unable to do anything but hold his wounded hand.

Now it's YOUR turn, Sneak!

»No, Bully!« yelled Koto. »We're not Rats! Just tie him up, and we can get out of here ...«

Bully turned his head. Koto had never seen him that furious before. Bully looked back at Sneak – and punched him so hard it made the walls shake.

He'll be easier to tie up now!

Koto and Bully hurried from the cave before the other Rats knew they had even been there. The moon was still up, as they climbed out of the sewers.

»Huh-thank you, buddy!« said Bully and gave Koto another bear hug.

»You too, Bully,« said Koto. »But what about you? Where will you stay now?«

»I've always dreamed of living in the country,« said Bully with a shy smile. »I think I would make a good farm boy!«

»Me too,« laughed Koto and shook his hand. »Good luck, Bully!«

By the power of
the clans!

It's true!
I was right!

Koto smiled proudly. »It's like I'm stronger, when I wear it ...«

»Of course, you fool!« said Gekko. »It's a TAYNIKMA!«

Koto had heard that name before, but still didn't know what it was.

»Listen, Koto ...« said Gekko. »Tayclania hasn't always been under the rule of the Empress. Once the land was free and a haven for caravans and trade ships. Anyone and anything could be found here!«

»Four clans ruled the land – the River Clan, the Mountain Clan, the Sun Clan and the Moon Clan. All clans had to agree to new laws, and any dispute was settled in large tournaments. Here the champions of each clan – the Taytans – would meet in duels.«

»Back then everyone had nikmas as tools or weapons, but Taytans would carry special ones with magical powers that represented their clan. These noble artefacts were known as Taynikmas. But the Empress knew their strength and destroyed nearly all of them, when she came into power!«

»How did she come into power?« asked Koto.

»That's a long and dark chapter of Tayclanian history,« said Gekko. »The clans each wanted more and more power, and that lead to a long war. Finally the clans made peace, though ...«

Gekko's face got dark. »But peace was fragile. A mighty champion of the Sun Clan tried to disrupt the treaty, and even though she was caught and banned from her clan, she didn't give up. She was gone for years, but returned with even greater and more terrible powers. Soon the land was hers ...«

But what about the Taytans?

She stole their souls and made them her Sentinels!

But change is coming ...

Gekko grabbed Koto by the arm and carefully touched the Taynikma.

»You think anyone will pay me 300 coins for it?«
asked Koto. »I mean, for my mum and dad ...«

Gekko gave Koto a stern look. »You want to sell it?
Could you bring yourself to do that?«

Koto was just about to nod – but then he felt a sharp
pang of doubt. The taynikma fit his wrist so perfectly. It
gave him so much strength. »Maybe I'm destined to wear
it,« thought Koto and looked up at Gekko.

»You're right,« he said. »I have to keep it!«

But I still have
to save my mum
and dad ...

»They're not the only ones you have to save,« said
Gekko. »Your task is much, much greater than that!«

See what
happens in
Book 3:
Tower of the Sun

No one can hide
from the crystal!

Perspective

You might remember this picture from Book 1: Master Thief, where a knome throws a "leaf" at Koto.

The leaf seems to be thrown out of the picture itself. That kind of depth is done with the use of perspective. If you want to draw difficult types of perspectives, it's always a good idea to draw the item in a box first.

The green lines are the ones that will point into the picture, when the leaf is drawn in perspective.

I'll start off by drawing the box in perspective and then fill in the leaf. Now I know the perspective is right.

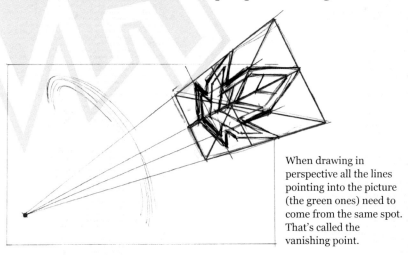

When drawing in perspective all the lines pointing into the picture (the green ones) need to come from the same spot. That's called the vanishing point.

Naturally the knome also needs a lot of speed lines and some cool colours. That will do the trick!

Model Sheets

When you make a series like Taynikma with many drawings, you're going to need a so-called "model sheet" for each of your main figures.

A model sheet is a kind of table where you place your full figure seen from the front, back and sideways. That way you will know what he looks like from any angle, and he will look the same in every picture.

1
2
3
4
5
6

Here's the model sheet for Koto in his new outfit.

Number of heads

When you draw a figure, you split him up into a "number of heads". Then you know how tall the entire body is. The red circles are each as tall as Koto's head. The entire body is then 6 "heads" tall.

Knowing that, it will be easier to draw his body the same height from picture to picture.

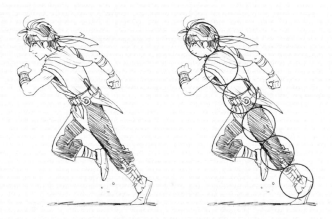

Colours

The model sheet will also show the colours used in that figure. Don't put too many in there. You will be colouring the figure many times, and the more colours he has, the longer it will take you.

This version of Koto consists of 8 different colours:

Twist your body

If you want the character you draw to look more dynamic, you will have to twist the body and head to face different directions.

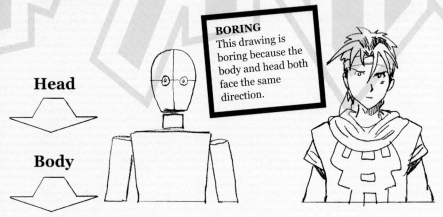

Head

Body

BORING
This drawing is boring because the body and head both face the same direction.

The drawing below is slightly better, as the body is now facing another direction. But it's still not really dynamic.

Head

Body

BETTER
But not quite good enough!

This is the way to do it!

The head is not facing the same direction as the body and notice how the eyes help create action, because they look in a third direction. To make the drawing even more dynamic we have tipped it forward. That gives you a sense of movement and action.

Eyes

Head

Body

LIKE THAT!
Now the drawing is dynamic. Body and head face different directions and we've tipped the body.

TAYNIKMA is a series of ten books!

Follow the adventures of Koto here:

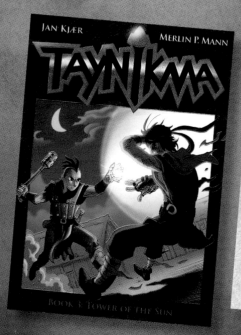

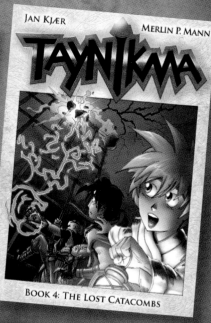

Book 3 and 4 will appear in August 2008
- ask at your local book dealer

Check for news and updates on our website
www.taynikma.co.uk